Vote for Isaiah!

A Citizenship Story

by Anastasia Suen
illustrated by Jeff Ebbeler

Content Consultant:
Vicki F. Panaccione, PhD
Licensed Child Psychologist
Founder, Better Parenting Institute

magic wagon

visit us at
www.abdopublishing.com

Printed in the United States.

Text by Anastasia Suen
Illustrations by Jeff Ebbeler
Edited by Patricia Stockland
Interior layout and design by Becky Daum
Cover design by Becky Daum

Library of Congress Cataloging-in-Publication Data

Suen, Anastasia.
  Vote for Isaiah! : a citizenship story / by Anastasia Suen ; illustrated by Jeff Ebbeler.
      p. cm. — (Main Street School. Kids with character)
  ISBN 978-1-60270-274-5
  [1. Elections—Fiction. 2. Citizenship—Fiction. 3. Schools—Fiction.] I. Ebbeler, Jeffrey, ill. II. Title.
  PZ7.S94343Vo 2008
  [E]—dc22
                                    2008002863

Isaiah walked down the hall with a poster in one hand and a roll of tape in the other.

"What are you doing?" asked Omar.

3

"I'm running for student council," said Isaiah.

"You're not running," said Omar. "You're walking."

"Funny," said Isaiah. "I'm walking in the hall. That's the rule, you know."

"I know," said Omar.

"But I *am* running for student council," said Isaiah.

"Why are you doing that?" Omar asked.

"I want to be on the student council to have a vote for our class," said Isaiah.

"That sounds like a good idea," said Omar. "Maybe you can vote for more recess!"

They both laughed.

"Well," said Isaiah, "I do want to be elected to help our class. And I guess more recess could help!"

"Hmm, maybe I can help you," said Omar. "Let me see your sign."

Isaiah held up his poster.

"Vote for Isaiah!" read Omar. He looked up at Isaiah. "That's it?"

"What?" said Isaiah.

"It needs more," said Omar.

"More?" asked Isaiah. "Like what?"

"Like, why people should vote for you,"
said Omar.

"Oh," said Isaiah. "Why should they vote
for me?"

"There are lots of reasons! Maybe the sign
should read: 'Vote for Isaiah! He's really
smart and friendly and honest,'" said Omar.

"But that's too much to put on a poster,"
said Isaiah.

"Okay," said Omar, shrugging. "How about, 'He's smart'? That will make students want to vote for you."

"You really think so?" asked Isaiah. "Where should I write it?"

Omar looked at the poster. "It will fit here at the bottom by your name."

"I need a marker," said Isaiah. "I have one in my desk."

"What color is it?" asked Omar.

"Blue," said Isaiah. "Why?"

"The rest of the poster is blue," said Omar. "It will all look the same. How about red?"

"I never thought of that," said Isaiah. "Good idea!"

"I really like art, just like my dad," said Omar.

"I have a big red marker in my desk that we can use," said Omar.

"Okay," said Isaiah.

The two boys walked back to the classroom.

"What is this?" said Omar. "There's a sign on our door."

"Grade 3! Vote for Melinda!" read Isaiah.

"She can't do that," said Omar.

"The office said I could put signs on doors and walls, too," said Isaiah.

"But she's not in our class," said Omar. "She's in Mrs. Johnson's class."

"Anyone in third grade can run for student council," said Isaiah.

"But we don't want her to win," said Omar. "We want you to win."

"Thanks," said Isaiah.

"Let's take down her sign," said Omar.

"I don't know . . .," said Isaiah.

"If I take down her sign," said Isaiah,
"will she take down mine?"

"Oh," said Omar. "That's a good point."
He looked at Melinda's sign.

"I just don't think it's right to take it down,"
said Isaiah. "It's her sign, not mine."

"But it's on our door," said Omar.

Isaiah sighed. "I know," he said. "But we want the vote to be fair. If we take down the sign, we won't know who the class really wants."

"I didn't think of that," replied Omar.

"Besides," Isaiah explained, "if I have to cheat to win, I probably don't deserve to be on student council anyway."

"I know! We can put my sign on their door," said Isaiah. "The kids in Mrs. Johnson's class can vote for me, too."

"That's why you need to win," said Omar. "You have good ideas."

Isaiah smiled.

"Let's get that red marker," said Omar. "I want you to represent our class!"

Isaiah and Omar opened the door and walked into the classroom.

"I only have one sign," said Isaiah. "I think I need to make more."

"I can help you," said Omar. He took the red marker out of his desk.

"Come over to my house after school," said Isaiah.

"I'll bring my art stuff," said Omar.

"Great!" said Isaiah.

What Do You Think?

1. Why did Isaiah want to put a poster in the hallway?

2. What do you think about Omar's advice to take down the sign?

3. Why did Isaiah leave Melinda's sign on Miss K's door?

Words to Know

cheat—to act dishonestly in order to win a game or get what you want.
council—a group of people chosen to look after the interests of others.
deserve—to be worthy of a reward or position.
election—the act or process of choosing someone or something by voting.
honest—being truthful and not lying or stealing or cheating.
represent—to act for someone or speak for other people.

Miss K's Classroom Rules

1. To be a good citizen, help others in need.
2. Treat others with respect by being honest.
3. Follow the rules, and don't cheat.
4. Vote!

Web Sites

To learn more about citizenship, visit ABDO Publishing Company on the World Wide Web at **www.abdopublishing.com**. Web sites about citizenship are featured on our Book Links page. These links are routinely monitored and updated to provide the most current information available.